SPEED DIALING

500-Word Flash Fiction

John A. Frederick

**Speed Dialing:
500-Word Flash Fiction**

Published by John A. Frederick

Address all inquiries to:
John A. Frederick
911 Central Avenue, Box 205
Albany, NY 12206
prosperitynowlifeofdreams@yahoo.com
www.johnafrederick.com

ISBN: 978-1-7351158-4-9 (paperback)
ISBN: 978-1-7351158-5-6 (e-book)
Library of Congress Control
Number: 2023915718

Editing: Superior Book Productions
Cover Design and Interior Book Layout:
Superior Book Productions
Author Photo Credit: Megan Thornburn

Every attempt has been made to properly source all quotes.

Printed in the United States of America

Dedication

To my muses: my family, my friends,
my lovers, my dogs, my beloved
Paris, and especially to my Higher
Power, Who loves and sustains me—
and us all.

Acknowledgments

Professor Joe Vallone, my community college English Literature professor, was an excellent and inspiring teacher and reader. Listening to him read excerpts from stories or poems in class made me want to write like he read.

Professor Joe Caruso taught a class on criminology and juvenile delinquency when I thought I might want to go into psychology, but he praised my papers, saying I should write for a living.

Special thanks to my editor, Tyler Tichelaar, and layout person, Larry Alexander, who put up with my quirks, questions, and stubbornness.

Contents

Introduction

I like boxes of words. In my youthful folly of college-romantic-poetry days, I found comfort in the structure of the sonnet, a box that was a definite size and shape. The words had to fit within the box for the sonnet to work. It is a fun puzzle—to make the words fit inside the box while having a complete thought and something to say. Being succinct doesn't come naturally to me.

I meticulously counted 500 words for each of these stories, but I won't be surprised if one or more of them don't hit my self-imposed (and admittedly compulsive) limit. No surprise....

I don't exactly know how I decided that 500 was the right number of words. I just decided. So, when I have an idea for a story, I usually don't know how it will end, but I do know where the end has to come. I feel safe in that awareness that this thing can't go on forever, or drift off into some wishy-washy dénouement, petering out at the end, uncertainly....

Most of the stories are true or based in some true event(s) that happened, either in my life or in history. The ones that are wholly fiction always surprise me in how they come to be. But even those based on my life held surprises for me.

Robert Frost wrote in "The Figure a Poem Makes," "....no surprise in the writer, no surprise in the reader. For me the initial delight is in the surprise of remembering something I didn't know I knew."

I hope you like my little boxes of surprise, my remembrances of something I didn't know.

John Frederick

Paris, France

Speed Dialing

Dewey hit redial.

There was an infinite pause, that immeasurable space between his finger releasing the button and the almost imperceptible change in the atmosphere of telephonic ambience that signaled the call was engaged.

Always, he both hated and relished that hesitation....the Prelude.

He *could* hang up. He never did.

Too late. Another click, and the connection was made. The other line began to ring....

Two rings. Three. Dewey had to remember to breathe. Four. The big click, and....

"You have reached Mayfield Savings and Loan. Please listen to the entire message before making a selection."

Dewey listened.

When he heard, "If you would like to speak to one of our agents, press five," he pressed five.

Another incipient pause. Growing. Deepening. Darkening. And then...Act One.

"Good afternoon. This is Evan. How may I help you?"

Hello, Evan. Personal contact was crucial.

"My name is Dewey V—. My account number is 123-456-7890 and my Lock Warning is ______________. I have a question about my account."

"Go ahead, sir."

"I see a bank fee for ten dollars because a check was returned. I would like that removed as a courtesy please." Dewey's breath was shallow. His heart was racing.

"Yes, sir. Thank you for being a valued customer. Could you repeat your full name and account number, please."

Dewey dutifully repeated his full name and account number. He had known that by saying it all in one breath that the customer service agent would *have* to ask him to repeat it.

His breath quickened imperceptibly as he waited for the Second Act.

"I see here a check did not clear on the twentieth and a service fee was charged."

Dewey raised his voice. "Yes, I said that. And I would like it removed *as a courtesy. Please!*"

Anger. Indignation. Impatience. Superiority over this minion on the other end of the phone. This servant whose salary he paid through his generous patronage and his *bank fees.*

"Yes, sir. One moment while I check your account."

Dewey sighed audibly. Loudly. Emphatically. The Entr'acte.

"Sir, I see you have had several overdraft charges removed in the past year, and many other requests. I count fifteen since January. We cannot possibly remove this charge."

This was Dewey's cue. Act Three.

Breath hot and heavy, heart racing, palms sweaty, his face flushed with excitement, raw energy, and rising ardor, he launched into the scene's climax.

Words flew from his lips. Spittle flew from his lips. His pupils dilated. His gorge rose....

The air turned blue. A torrent of curse words. Vile, foul. Unspeakable.

The poor agent. Victim of Dewey's fevered obsession. Unsuspecting.

It was all the agent could do to gather his wits and abruptly terminate the call.

Dewey, blind with rage, did not notice at first that the other end of the line had gone dead. When he did, he stopped in mid-curse. Stopped dead, like a bug hits a windshield.

He had not finished.

His naked body trembled.

He could not *not* redial.

Under the Prairie Moon

A T NIGHT, THE land seemed under a spell. Inside the small circle of wagons, a smaller circle of firelight. Outside those circles...nothing.

Blackness swept upward on all sides, rising into an upturned bowl of countless stars. The waxing moon above the eastern horizon would watch over these pioneers all night. The sky after midnight would be graced by shooting stars, the time of year known to the Original Ones as the Nights of the Little Tears. The crystal lights appeared and disappeared quickly. Sometimes, a single tear, sometimes, many clustered together. The streaks they left behind lingered long on the mind of one's eye....

Passing by the wagon train's travelers, huddled around their small fire, were a quiet and purposeful band of Native People moving, no more than shadows in the blackness. They had no reason to be seen, and so they were not. They had soft feet, as did their ponies; their children knew silence as well as they knew their own names. Their infants would not cry nor fuss for any reason, knowing the safety of quietude. The True People were heading south to better lands before the grasses browned and the wind shifted to the bitter North; the wind's cry came long and loud and steady from the Land of Great Snows.

The campfire dwindled; the stars wheeled west. The Polar Star was an unmoving center of all that had been and all that would be. Keeping close to their circle of dying light, the pioneers did not talk much.

The journey had already taken weeks. Weeks lay ahead. The monotony weighed heavily. Nothing yet had stirred to break it.

They would pray for this dull and aching sameness soon enough, when days later a whirling wind as tall as ten trees came dropping out of the dark clouds, taking up one of the party, never to be seen nor heard from again.

And again, that very same week, they would pray when thunder shook the ground. Came *from* the ground. A sustained rumbling that had no origin and no direction. All around, all at once...until, on the horizon, a tremendous herd of horned and hump-backed creatures came toward them. Stretching from left to right as far as the eye could see, the creatures came with hooves pounding, dust and air and grasses and clods of dirt all flying in and around and above the relentless onslaught, coming ever closer with no sane way for the travelers to understand, nor to flee, nor to fight until—at what seemed like the last second and, in fact, was quite likely so—the herd turned as if on command and headed parallel to the travelers, leaving them breathless, dazed, and exhausted as if they had, in fact, been trampled.

Their souls had been trampled and would be again and again in days to come. Under the prairie moon, which each night waned to an awful emptiness, they would see things and live things nobody back East would ever believe....

A Good Death

The knock at the door was faint, but I heard it clearly.

Or did I? Was it a dream?

Clearly? Faintly? That made no sense.

I had been dozing in the chair, how long? Book on my lap.

"Hello?" No answer.

"Hello? Hello? Come in...."

The knob jiggled. Muffled through the door, an unfamiliar voice said, "It's locked."

"It's not," I replied. "Hold on."

I struggled to get up from the easy chair. My left leg had fallen asleep. Pins and needles. I couldn't put any weight on it.

The knock. Again. Louder.

"Hold on! Hold on!"

Who could this be? At this hour.

I sighed and rose. I found my cane and steadied myself before starting the voyage across the carpet, an ancient threadbare but beautiful rug my grandmother once had shipped back home from India on one of her many trips abroad.

She and my grandfather traveled the world on tramp steamers, a way of travel that is long since gone. On cargo ships there were cabins for maybe a dozen passengers. You'd be gone for months on a loose itinerary, depending on the vagaries of port schedules and captains' whims.

And unlike air travel, you could easily bring back your own cargo.

Once, they shipped a VW Bug—which they first drove around Europe—bought from the VW factory in Karmann, Germany—a factory now long shuttered.

The cargo ships' passengers made their own fun in those pre-internet days: card games, parlor games, etc., they took turns hosting cocktail parties and spent long hours writing journal and diary entries, and letters home, to be mailed in bulk at the next port.

Or reading. Or watching the ocean, looking for dolphins, or flying fish, or whales.

Their ship, just passed through the Panama Canal, was steaming north of Cuba. It was after dinner. The sun setting behind them.

On the deck, in their chairs, the lazy days would soon be over. Two days until they landed home, after an extensive voyage down the west coast of South America.

Papa got up from his chair and went to the railing. The sun had just slipped below the horizon and Venus, goddess of Love, shone brightly in the west.

He sighed.

In a quiet voice, to my grandmother, to himself, and to the sky, he quoted Tennyson:

> *Sunset and evening star,*
> *And one clear call for me!*

> *And may there be no moaning*
> *of the bar,*
> *When I put out to sea,*

And he collapsed into his chair and died.

My poor grandmother had to finish the voyage alone, Papa's body in the ship's cold storage until they reached New Jersey.

I had just about made it to the door when my left leg, still all pins and needles, gave out from under me and I hit the deck.

The knob rattled loudly, turned, and the door opened.

"Told you it was unlocked." Surprisingly, that made us both laugh.

My visitor extended a hand.

"Time to put out to sea."

Sweet Peach Juice

W**HAT DID SHE** think was going to happen, sweet peach juice running down her wrist and arm and chin and onto her white T-shirt in the summer afternoon sun with us boys taking a break from our labors along the road, and it hot and all, and that jug of water just didn't go around enough times before it was dry, did it?

The mown hay only made things worse, smelling sweet and grassy, thick and earthy, and musky. A thousand summer insects buzzing in the heat—crickets and honeybees and cicadas and katydids—buzzing con-stant, air vibrating.

This steady hiss had a counter-point: the sound of blade on grass, the rhythmic whack whack whack of the scythes on the tall grass, times twenty. But when we got the cadence in unison—the sound was true.

Resting now, all was good, and though there was no shade here, just to sit and sweat and breathe easy was enough. And though, as I said, the jug got emptied too soon, time to ourselves was worth more than just about anything.

Then She happened.

Then She happened by, happened by in her rattletrap truck sputtering with the choke valve closed too tight so as she stalled. Stalled right here.

She got out of the truck. Boss didn't move, but he didn't have to. He scoped everything, slow and quick at once, if you know what I mean. He gave us all a look, and we knew, without saying a thing, to set and stay set.

"Ma'am?"

"Seems I have a little engine problem," She said. Never heard a voice that sounded helpless and confident at once.

"Ma'am?"

Boss didn't move. But one eye moved, and it lit on me. I can fix anything.

Got up slow and quick if you know what I mean. Unlatched the hood to peer in at the Willys. It was a Hurricane engine, and to be honest,

I knew what the problem was before she ever even stopped, but why rush?

Meanwhile, She, looking helpless and confident, ambled around the side of the Willys and tossed back the green tarpaulin. She was haulin' peaches into town, baskets full.

She took one and looked at it, turning it 'round and 'round before she bit into that sweet thing. I saw it all even with my head buried deep under the hood. Oh yes, I did, and I heard the munch of the peach, teeth on skin, and smelt the juices, ripe-just-enough ripe.

"You boys want a peach? Can these boys have a peach?"

I made noise like I was fixing something.

Boss never before appeared like he appeared just then. Confident and puzzled, weight shifting from one foot to th'other.

She took another bite, sweet peach juice running down her wrist and arm and chin and onto her white T-shirt. Sweet, sweet peach juice in the afternoon.

Thirty-eight eyes looked at She, then at Boss. Nineteen men got up in unison. My two eyes stayed fixed on the choke.

The Winning

SPRING WAS COLDER than we had hoped. After a long winter, wet and dark, we longed for sun and hints of blossoms on the trees in the Luxembourg Gardens.

Wrapped in my coat and scarf, I hastened from the doorway at 27 rue de Fleurus, my path bisecting the gardens.

The wind was biting, the lights flickering on, the gardens nearly deserted, my hands buried in my pockets, and my thoughts straining to stay on, and stay off, the conversation that had ended abruptly five minutes ago with me putting my manuscript deep in my jacket, nodding a nod to Alice, and storming out.

"*Inaccrochable,*" she said, handing me back my life's sweat. *Unpublishable!*

All thoughts of light, all thoughts that are good, that are friendly, warm, inviting, happy. Banished. A plate of oysters and a nice white; wrestling or swimming or skiing or tennis and—whatever sport—winning; sitting in the café, the words just coming; taking the train, or a steamer... somewhere, anywhere; mounting the stairs to home, dinner waiting. The dark mood would not allow them, allow these thoughts, sunny and warm, to penetrate.

Who do I need? What do I need? What do I care? Only the work. Only the fight. Only the winning.

Through the gardens, walking faster, gray sky almost black, yet west, at my back, space has opened between cloud and sky. I see sunlight reflected on the dome of the Panthéon.

The light golden white. And bright, not because it was brilliant, but because we have suffered weeks of cold gray with nearly no hint of blue, of sun.

Forced now into my field of vision, I cannot decide. Friend or foe this light? Does it mock me at my back, compelling me to turn to confront it directly? Or is it gently approaching at an oblique angle aslant, to remind me of better days behind, and yet to come?

Far from dispelling it, the sunlight amplifies my dark mood, giving it a contrasting starkness. Walking helps, but this is not a race that can be won in a sprint. Winning here is enduring, sustaining, holding out. Patience.

Now the Panthéon. The dead greats of France entombed. Entombed, honored and great. Past the Université Paris Sorbonne where students scurry into the dark to cafés to discuss great ideas over Pernod, in dreams of absinthe.

The Place de la Contrescarpe; home yards away and the three flights up to light and warmth. And Hadley.

Entering the Place, I see the familiar hill, down the rue Cardinal Lemoine.

Suddenly, a bundle of green rags in a doorway startles me.

"Excusez-moi, monsieur. Quelques sous pour une pauvre âme assoiffée."

I see him. I hear him. Though my French is poor, I understand him.

This one has surrendered. His fight is over, which is to say his *will* to fight is over. Lost.

Bah! I throw coins at the rags. Who do I need? What do I care?

Only the work. Only the fight. Only the winning.

Down Truckee Lake

"ARE YOU MEN from California, or do you come from heaven?"

Levinah could not see, not properly. What she could make out were several shapes—maybe a dozen—brown and blurred against the infinite whiteness.

She squinted, but it did not help. There was nary a break between sky and ground. Just sameness, white on white for days on days. The snow blindness had come weeks ago. It left during long days indoors, stormy days of never-ending snows, but reappeared quickly on outside days, days like today, rare days of blue sky and clear air.

Of a sudden this morning, these silent shapes appeared, smudges lumbering slowly out of the white void, from down Truckee Lake. She had been gathering snow to melt for water and cutting strips of the cabin's rancid ox hide roof to boil and eat.

She heard her own words, but perhaps she had not spoken aloud, for there was no immediate answer. Perhaps they *were* from heaven and had no need of speech. Perhaps her body—barely corporeal, hair near gone, teeth near gone, paper-thin skin, white as snow—had trans-formed. Perhaps the physical had be-come ethereal.

Perhaps heaven was like this: no pain, no cold, no hunger. Blindness, yes, but she *could* see, in ways that needed not eyes.

For instance, she had seen Charles Stanton visit one night, which was odd because he had left with the party of men who went off on snowshoes to attempt to cross the mountain pass and fetch help. He had said nothing but looked at her so mournful sad. She had risen to greet him, but he shook his head sorrowfully and quietly drifted up the smoke-hole.

Twice more it happened on successive nights. Poor Patrick Dolan was a fearful sight, pale white, naked, and with a fearsome grimace on his face, like unto a man possessed by demons.

And saddest of all, her own boy, her own Lemuel Murphy, just turned twelve that fall. His face a mask of calm, he alone of the three approached near enough for her to touch. His hand reached her face, stroked her cheek, her hair.

The whisper was felt more than heard. *Ma. I'm a- goin' home now*. She wanted to hug him and she moved to, but he halted her with a glance, and she flinched back.

Lemuel, she thought, *what is to become of us now?* as if he held some secret prophecies in his intermediate state. Something like unto a smile, a ghost of a smile, crossed his face, briefly and like a candle, flickered out, so as not to give too much light, too much hope.

His eyes were neither hard nor soft, looking neither pitying nor comforting. Then he dissolved into nothingness, and the blackness of the cabin was absolute.

Now, outside, three smaller shapes broke away, dancing circles, feeble but happy. George Donner's children. "We are saved!" they chorused.

The reply floated to her: "Ma'am, we come up from the valley; Sacramento."

Moving Day

"**S**HE'S NOT HAPPY here, can't you see?"

The three of us gathered around our mother, who gave no indication that we were even there.

"But...but moving her is crazy! It doesn't make sense."

My sensible sister. Sober and to the point. She drove the farthest and wasn't too happy to give up her weekend after working a sixty-hour week.

I felt for her, saw how torn she was. Practical versus sentimental.

The ancient war—head and heart—played out in her body language.

Eventually, she'd see—and do—what was right.

"What do you think?" I asked my brother, the middle one. He has a great head on his shoulders, but, as someone once said, he wouldn't say *shit* if he had a mouthful.

"I dunno." He drew a drag on his cigarette. "I mean...she's been here a long time, but...."

I finished his thought, "but nobody visits her. Nobody lives here anymore. You're way up north, I'm moving to France, and...."

"I live out of state, but even if I lived closer, I would never come here. I hate this place," my sister finished the sentence.

I hate this town.

My sister's antipathy for our hometown was more than justified. After Mom left, Dad remarried. His new wife behaved just like the proverbial wicked stepmother, miserly measuring out cereal and shampoo while they both doted on her children. We two older brothers had mercifully bailed out of that gin-and-vodka-soaked home by then.

Mom was still, and we were no closer to a decision.

It was her loneliness, her isolation I felt most deeply. I just knew she was miserable.

Maybe I was projecting my feelings, but because she couldn't articulate her desires, I had to base our choice on my gut instinct.

"If you think you hate it here, think about what Mom would want," I implored. "Here she is, day after day, no friends around, nobody visits...." I began to well up, but I composed myself and continued.

"Look at these flowers. How long have they been here? Dead. Dry....

"....and the way they treat her...." They had just moved someone in right next to her. And now with a total stranger, it seemed like she was even more alone, if that could be possible.

"It's...it's...time," I concluded. "Let's move her away from here. Back home, down to where she grew up. All her family is there. She...."

I trailed off, overcome with the enormity of the situation, of where

Dad had put her and left her, him getting remarried and each of us going our own ways.

I *was* projecting all right. Projecting *my* feelings of guilt, *my* regret eating at me. It was *my* dereliction that was moving me to make this desperate, foolish, impractical, necessary decision: to move her back home, to where her parents, grandparents, aunts, uncles, and siblings were. All happy and nearby to each other.

I turned to my brother and sister. "Are we agreed?"

They nodded.

Tell them to start digging.

À FRÉD. CHOPIN

Chopin's Heart

T HE STRINGS BEGIN the march, low, sonorous. The tuba forms the floor underneath, its laborious notes drifting drearily, a slow, heavy fog across damp ground. The other horns wait reluctantly. The cold wind whips the hem of black cloaks, and men touch a soft hand to their top hats. Late October, brown leaves swirl. The gray sky threatens but doesn't move, doesn't open, solemnly honoring the moment unfolding below. The women's dresses, also black, rustle quietly as the orchestra takes its time with forlorn patience. The crowd is much smaller than the thousands gathered earlier outside *la Madeline*. The orchestra's strains cannot be heard clearly by those on the edge.

Now the strings lift. The trees respond, letting the gods know they too stand in witness. Nearer the grave, the circle of mourners stand stock still, heads bowed. Over them, Euterpe weeps, holding her broken lyre as a mother would hold a baby who had just succumbed to gentle death — with sorrow, resignation. A void in the world that will never close. The funeral march rises in a billowing eddy of strings and tenor horns, emulating the wind, or the soul as it breaks free and leaves the heavy bass-note of its body for the freedom of the sky.

His sister, most bereft of those bereft, holds the oaken urn close to her. "Tears fall at night, but joy comes in the morning," she says quietly.

Scarcely hearing the music, in her mind she hears another tune. The Nocturne, the *Night Piece* he wrote for her, which she has heard but which the world will not hear, will not hear for two decades more. *"To my sister Ludwika as an exercise before beginning the study of my second Concerto,"* he wrote.

These are the notes that echo in her mind, that rise and swell. *No!* she thinks, fighting to overcome the *March Funèbre*. He is not dead! He will not be dead! He will live! She impels the Nocturne in C# minor, forcing it out from her mind, out into the ether, impelling it forward in time—

Into the future, she sends it with the Force of Light. One hundred years....

"Play," he commanded.

She played.

"You will live," the Commandant declared after she finished.

"Not without my sister," she said, in a determined, jaw-defiant whisper.

Chopin's sister at his graveside, by force of will alone, sends the unheard Nocturne to Poland...to Kraków-Plaszów...to the death camp. The music *will* be played on a piano behind barbed wire searchlights and stone hearts.

Beautiful. Perfect. Sanctified.

The *Night Piece* will play once again, again to save another life…in the ghetto.

It is destined for this. Now he is dead. Dead at thirty-nine. Yet the piece he wrote has more than Life in it, more than God's Love, to save the world.

Ludwika will leave for Warsaw that very night, back to Poland, secretly. In oak encased, Chopin's heart, carried back to Poland, country of his birth that he will never see again….

The Ground Will
Break Her Fall

THE DOOR CREAKED. Shit!

"Fannie? Is that you?"

"Yes, Granny." I sighed. "I'm going out for some fresh air."

"Oh, that's good. Fresh air is healthy," comes a voice out of the dark like dry leaves.

Some fresh air was a quick hour in Smitty's neighborhood bar.

Only three months living here, and I was already off my promise to myself.

To break the cycle. To drink only on weekends. Or special occasions.

To not sleep with someone on the first date.

Living with Granny wasn't ideal, but it was free. All I had to do was care for her.

That was "all."

That was a lot.

Foot out the door, I turned back into the darkness of the "parlor," as Granny called it, where the hospital bed was set square in the middle with the low hiss of the oxygen.

Quietly, I looked by the glow of my phone to see the old woman asleep already. The drugs worked.

An hour…or two. No more. She's fine. It's just down the street.

I slipped out into the cool spring air, moist. Pungent earth after a long Buffalo winter. It smelled like something on the verge.

The sidewalks glistened with the melting snowbanks, now sad remnants of their former February greatness. This winter especially had seen the Lake Erie Snow Machine churning foot after foot of lake effect snows, like the ones that usually hit north of here, along the Tug Hill.

It was only two blocks and a right, and neon had such a powerful allure, yellow and green with a slight buzzing flicker. I tasted the anticipation.

The door stuck so you had to yank hard. Inside, the smell. Definitely not springtime, but wood and popcorn and faintly men's cologne. The Alley Cats Shuffle Puck bowling machine rang gaily as one of the players racked up a strike.

"Hi, Smitty." I smiled at the bartender. "Granny's out, and I am too!"

Smitty looked up from the sink where he was sudsing pony glasses. "You have exactly ten seconds to turn your ass around and get the hell out of here."

"What...?"

He seemed so angry I thought he was gonna hurl the beer glass in his hand at my head.

"What...what do ya mean?"

He made a move like he was going to come around the bar quick. I couldn't think. I turned and hit the door. Burning tears, burning cheeks....

Smitty watched her leave—fast! And that was the last he hoped to see of her.

The five-alarm fire in his brain cooled down as quickly as it had ignited, and he ambled back to the sink. Solly looked up slightly from his beer glass. He had to cup it with both hands to lift it to his lips.

"She's a wild one, yessiree."

"Wild? Capital T trouble. I don't need that."

"Think she got the hint?"

"Can't tell." He wiped his hands on the bar rag at his waist.

"Maybe so…. If she remembers in the morning."

The Willow

THE WEEPING WILLOW stood in the backyard taller than the suburban one-story house.

Summer and winter, fall and spring, its pendulous branches formed a flowing curtain that almost touched the ground. Its narrow leaves shivered in the slightest breeze.

Its lowest branch was just too high—a half a hand too high for a six-year-old boy, who try as he might, could not snag it, even with his mightiest jump.

"If you can't get up yourself, you don't belong up there," Dad said in response to the boy's pleadings.

Summer turned to fall and the boy's birthday party under the tree was cake and friends and presents and Mom. It never occurred to the boy to pull a chair up to the tree to give himself a boost.

That winter, the Great Ice Storm came. His dad went out in the freezing rain to light a bonfire under the willow. This made the boy worry. Won't the tree burn up? "The heat will melt the heavy ice on the branches so that she doesn't fall under the weight" Dad said.

The boy didn't know the tree was a "she."

Spring came and with it baseball, which the boy liked, but he had no gift for hitting a ball or throwing a ball. Alone, he walked through the fields behind the house to the Little League park, but the best he could do was buy some candy from the concession stand and watch without a glove.

Trudging back home through the fields, he practiced throwing rocks, but gave up after a few mis-thrown tries. In the backyard, he checked on the tree. The lowest branch. Was it lower? He jumped and….

His right hand snagged and held on. His feet were (maybe) an inch off the ground. Now what?

He pulled himself up and his left hand managed to grip the branch too. But it was wide, and his hands were small. Both hands slipped. The rough, gray bark left a mark and burning palms.

Again…. Right hand. Left hand. Hanging in mid-air. Now what?

Feet.

He managed to swing his legs up. The soles of his PF Flyers gripped the bark. Walking up the trunk, he hooked his leg over the branch.

Now what?

Pull! Pull with all your might: two hands, two arms, and a leg all together working in a new cooperative effort. Add in some momentum, swinging hips and torso and….

Sitting on the branch. The lowest branch.

Mom! Look!

Mom glanced out of the kitchen window.

Suddenly, angry, worried and terrified, she burst out from the back door.

"Get down! You'll hurt yourself."

The boy loved his mother. Even at seven, he sensed she was different than other moms, but he wasn't sure how. There were things he knew that she just didn't know.

He smiled at her and started to wave, but a sudden wave of fear hit him as he almost let go.

He realized he would need both hands steady to climb higher.

The Forgotten Winchester

Vraiment Beau tipped his hat and looked into the sun.

Set up on the western side of the canyon, with only one way in and one way out, anybody looking for him would have the sun blazing in their eyes…for two hours anyhow.

After that, it would be too dark. Nobody would venture into the arroyo, and as long as he kept no fire, he would have a peaceful night.

Horse watered and fed, he ate cold beans and pemmican he made himself from dried Utah serviceber-ries. He ate slow and drank slower, keeping his eyes all the while on the dry wash that bent out of sight in the shrubs and pinyon pines, the sage-brush, juniper, and jimson weed.

After he ate and before the sun disappeared, he laid out his bedroll, and after cleaning his guns, he'd treat himself to a smoke. A cigarette glow-ing in the dark would be foolish, but before sunset, the smell of smoke? That's a chance he would take.

Soon the sun would leave the canyon in deep shadow, then in darkness. He had just reassembled the Winchester and was stowing the cleaning gear when his horse shift-ed and gave a nervous whinny. She scented something.

But what? Shawna didn't spook easily, so a rabbit or a rattler heading home to its hole wouldn't startle her. No, this was something that needed further investigation.

He leaned the rifle against a juniper tree and drew his Colt.

He heard nothing. Saw nothing. The sun hit the canyon's rim. The sharp line between light and shadow drifted along the canyon floor and up its sides.

Vraiment Beau crouched down, under cover of shade and scrub pine, eyes scanning, ears attuned to anything that signaled location, presence, size, or intention of the person or party, such as it was.

Shawna snorted and pawed the ground with her hoof shaking her reins. Suddenly, darkness....

The Winchester '73 stood against the juniper all that year and into the next. The heavy Nevada winter snows covered her completely in deep drifts wafted up by the wind.

The next spring and the next and the next passed. The sun rose and set. The moon rose and set, its fickle phases shifting.

The horse bolted and was long gone. A prospector came, salvaging what gear was still salvageable, but he never saw the rifle leaning against the tree.

The Forgotten Winchester rusted, waited. She alone knew what happened to Vraiment Beau, witnessed the cowboy searching the dark, crouching low, using all his survival senses, instincts that had saved him in card games, on long trail rides moving cattle, and the occasional romantic interlude that he always managed to rein back when things got too serious.

Only the Winchester saw the blinding bright lights above, heard the unknown whirr, felt the rush of wind and energy as Vraiment lifted skyward, arms dangling, Colt in his hand, yellow-green whirling lights pulsating, whooshing upward, quickly vanishing, a pinpoint in the bright starlit western sky.

The Same Moon

HE CALLED HER

    She answered

Hi

Hi

What are you doing

Just nothing

In bed

What are you doing

I had a thought so I needed to call
you right away before it seemed silly

A thought

Yeah a thought but you'll think it's silly

Probably

What was it

Are you in your bedroom

Yes

Go to the window and look out

Really

Just do it

Hold on

Ok I'm looking

Whaddya see

I don't see anything

*I see the neighbors left their poor dog
outside again*

I'm going to call the cops

Well, look up

What

Look up

Do you see the moon

Yes

It's a full moon and a blue moon
and a super moon all at once

Isn't she beautiful

*I can see it's full but why is it blue
and why is it super*

It's blue because it's the second
moon this month

It's super because it is closer than normal so it seems much bigger than normal

Isn't she lovely

It is pretty but you got me out of bed for that

I had a thought

You said that

You thought I should see the pretty big super moon

So now I've seen it

That wasn't the thought

Oh

What was your thought

Are you still looking at the moon

Yes, she lied

I'm looking at it here and you're looking at it there

We're looking at the same moon at the same time

Isn't that romantic

Uh-huh

It connects us both from 225,000 miles away

It shines its light on your face into your eyes at the exact same moment it shines into mine

Uh-huh

No wonder people have thought of the moon and of romance for centuries

You're not going to quote that Shakespeare again are you

I wasn't but I can

Please don't

It's late I'm tired

*I was just about to turn the light out
when you called*

I almost didn't answer

I'm glad you did though

Think of it

The same moon

*Yes it is a nice thought and I'm glad
you shared it with me*

I wish I was there

Well you aren't

*You're in San Francisco instead of
here in Seattle*

I know that you aren't happy with the long distance thing

Well you wanted to try it and so we're trying it

A six-month experiment to see if I like the job and if we're able to navigate the logistics

The logistics yes

So far so good don't you think

I have to think about that and you should have talked to me before deciding to move to Frisco

We discussed it

You decided before we discussed it

Yeah I guess

I had a pretty good idea I wanted to take the job but

*You can't say we discussed if you'd
pretty much made up your mind now
can you*

I guess not

But so far so good don't you think

I gotta go

Ok good night

Good night

You coming back to bed?

In a sec

A Week
at the Beach

CAN WE GO look at the beach?

Our first day in Florida, bright mid-February sunshine. Our northern New York winter coats stowed in the car, mom toting our baby sister.

Dad had an idea: "Boys, first get our things in the room. The beach isn't going anywhere."

Reluctantly, we dragged feet back to the station wagon and took a suitcase and a bag.

The room smelled like Florida, a strange land with hanging Spanish Moss and a palm tree right outside our room. We snorted when the roadside diner waitress called Mom, "Honey," asking, "Y'all want grits, right?"

We didn't.

The drive down, generally boring, was made easier with car games (counting license plates, counting cows) and moments of surprise—

A billboard outside of Winston-Salem—a white-hooded Klansman on a blood-red horse rearing menacingly against a black background.

The noxious stench in Georgia, like nothing I've ever smelled before or since.

The armadillo meandering through our campsite. Mom screamed and jumped up on the picnic table.

Sad chain gangs in the heat, weed-whacking along the roadside with scythes.

The memories seared on my brain….

Next day mid-morning: blinding white sand, gray-green ocean, hazy blue sky, billowing ship-like clouds sailing the horizon. Sunlight bouncing off the sea in diamonds.

We had our trunks. My brother and I hit the water with a splash. Hours of salty joy in ocean waves, with short breaks for pretzels and Tang swigged from the camping jug, and later, sandy sandwiches Mom packed.

We had rafts too. Dad, a pipe smoker, spent his wind blowing them up. Lying face down, Mother Ocean swelling underneath, felt erotic and hypnotic. I am fourteen.

Afternoon, the folks, under their umbrella, in their chairs with their own jug and plastic cups, kept half an eye on us. We were experienced swimmers, and we lived in a time before parents were helicopters.

That evening, we were tuckered out to say the least and slept soundly, happily after the full, full day.

Fire in the morning. My fair-haired brother couldn't open his eyes. He lay on the bed moaning. Hallucinating.

I couldn't move my arms, legs; my stomach, chest, back intense with heat. The redness was boiled-lobster red; the pain virtually unbearable.

Calamine lotion was virtually useless—and since aloe gel hadn't been invented yet, we suffered in the dark hotel room, curtains drawn, cool washcloths and nothing else.

Television held no interest, although we left it on. The folks checked on us from time to time. Nobody thought to call a doctor.

Three days (or was it four?) in the room in the dark in agony.

Finally, the blisters subsided, and the world slowly returned to "normal." Normal.

There would be no more swimming this Florida vacation, no going outside without long-sleeved shirts and a hat—especially for my fair-haired brother.

I can't remember anything ever being said or this registering as a significant event in anyone's mind but ours.

A week at the beach. The memory seared on my brain….

A Family Bridge

WHENEVER MY DAD'S relatives got together, they ended up pulling out the card table and playing a few rubbers of bridge. We kids were allowed to watch... quietly.

"No kibitzing," my grandfather growled, cigar stub in his teeth. Whenever he played Diamonds, he called them, "Demons."

My grandmother, the foursome's only Life Master, played a quiet, methodical game. Dad was a nervous player, and Mom—a high school graduate among PhDs and an Italian among Ukrainian Jews—was already out of her element even before game-ly trying to learn the game.

Once a year, my grandmother's Uncle Al came to town, with his booming voice and huge laugh. He called me, *Giovanni*. I wished my parents had the wisdom to give me that exotic name. *Giovanni!*

Al wrote for radio quiz shows in the 1940s and had an endless stream of trivia questions for us. The easy ones earned a penny or a nickel; harder ones a fifty-cent piece, or even a dollar....

As he drank more, the questions—and the money—grew. We strained to name as many presidents (in order) as we could or close our eyes and name twenty things in the living room, a room we spent every day of our lives in, but never studied closely.

We'd easily walk away with twenty dollars—big money in 1968!

Al played piano by ear, old tunes and college fight songs rolling off the keys. Al sang the loudest and my mother the sweetest, with her beautiful voice. She dreamed of being a cabaret singer, a dream which, alas, never came true.

Al's "job" was tournament director for the American Contract Bridge League. After retiring as the league's director and handing the reins to his nephew, Jerry, Al spent months at sea on ocean liners. He ran bridge tournaments on world cruises, sending us postcards from all over. He knew I collected stamps.

Later in life, I realized I was a scion among bridge "royalty." Al's sister, my great-grandmother Sadie, was secretary to the Bridge League. Al's first wife, Helen, was a chorus girl in the Marx Brothers' Broadway show *Animal Crackers*, where Chico taught her how to play bridge (and who knows what else?).

She and Al hobnobbed with the Broadway elite of 1930s Manhattan, people like Cole Porter. She became Charles Goren's favorite partner. When asked what it was like to play with the greatest bridge player in the world, Helen replied, "Ask Charles."

When Al's favorite nephew Jerry became director of the bridge league, he and Aunt Trudy played bridge and taught the game to a slew of Washington, DC ambassadors, politicians, bureaucrats, and even a president or two. I have an autographed photo of Eisenhower, an avid bridge player with Uncle Al at a tournament in DC.

Who knew that those informal (yet very serious) after-dinner bridge games when my grandparents were in town were a bridge to Bridge history and family ancestry all at once?

I still wish my parents had named me *Giovanni*....

My Own Private Stonehenge

I CAN TIME THE exact date of the spring and fall equinox by using the Paris Métro.

Métro lines 6 and 2 trace a smile and a frown respectively across the face of Paris. These are the only lines that run above ground. They follow the ancient path of the eighteenth-century Wall of the Farmers General, which once surrounded the city.

Line 2 loops north from the Porte Dauphine to the Place de Nation. Line

6 curls south, from the Place Charles de Gaulle—Étoile and the Arc de Triomphe, ending also at Nation.

The wall was not a defensive fortification but a customs barrier to keep untaxed goods from coming into the city. The many city *portes* were manned by tax agents inspecting goods and levying import duties. Villages like Montmartre flourished because of their cheaper goods—notably wine, making Montmartre a favorite of penniless artists.

But I digress.

My apartment sits near the foot of métro Line 6 at Passy station. My *salon* windows on the *rez de chaussée* face northeast. With another apartment building directly across the street, the rising sun shines obliquely in my windows—once it is up.

In summer, that is quite early, although I am still asleep and the *volets* are still closed. In winter, the sun rises late, as late as 8:30 on those darkest days before Christmas.

Especially in the days of COVID, my couch was my writing desk, Zoom meeting space, meal space, and streaming video space. I live on my couch, my dog Manny Morkie constantly beside me, sister Erica across the room on her preferred pillow, coming over to give kisses or get petted.

So, I sit on my couch—winter dark or summer brilliance, and just twice a year, a phenomenon happens for just a few short days. Which at first startled me....

At my computer at 8:00 a.m., I was looking at the quilt of faces on a

Zoom recovery meeting screen, listening to heartfelt and soul-healing sharing, when I suddenly noticed a subtle shift in the light, as though someone had put a dimmer switch on the sun. Then, just as suddenly, the light returned.

Perhaps my imagination? A small stroke? Soon, it happened again. Unmistakably this time.

Getting up from my couch, I went over to the window. The sun was fine, shining brightly on a fall morning. Perhaps a trick of my eyes. Then….

I saw the métro, the Line 6 train heading across the Seine. Line 6, my line with its spectacular view of the Eiffel Tower on its way across the river Seine as it headed toward Passy and beyond to the Trocadero.

And look! The train is eclipsing the sun on its way across the bridge.

Sun and sky, train and tracks all positioned perfectly in alignment with my windows. No other apartment, I venture, has this exactly perfect configuration.

Twice a year, at the fall and spring equinox, the métro recreates an ancient Neolithic phenomenon: My Own Private Stonehenge.

The Dreaming

DREAMS ARE BECOMING clearer. Clearly I am ready.

Shapes shimmer just below the surface of my slowly-waking consciousness, dark shapes gliding beneath dark waters, swimming. Occasionally surfacing.

I can see them—murky, yes. Clearer, nonetheless.

Upon awakening, the placid green-gray waters recede. I wish to remain asleep/awake, but the morning washes over me. I struggle to keep my place as the scene dissolves to day.

However, I can recall vaguely the mysterious life that lies submerged below. Giants. Big, black hulks of shipwrecks, mermaids, angels, whales, and sharks. And treasure.

Shadows, slightly darker than the dark water, shadows swimming, floating, drifting. Lying on the bottom. Now looming large.

What are they?

Who are they?

Despair and hope always to swim together. Always run together.

I wish my dreams to be clear, crisp and clean and cutting-edge sharp, bringing me to other worlds, visiting other maestros, seeing new colors, learning old truths.

Once I ran with wolves.

I need these nightly reveries. I need these nightly horse rides, the pale horse riding swiftly on wings across the bright-silver full moon, beyond the thin veil of this world to the next world.

From the depths to the heights, I implore the gatekeeper: let me pass.

If ever a man needed to be transported to the healing lands, that man is I.

In this world, the sameness is palpable—daily. While it is enough for me, this world being what it is....

Yet I know there is more. One has heard tales. Once, twice, many times, I *have* seen beyond. I know *it* is there—as easy to reach as this cup of coffee here on the table before me.

I pick it up and sip. Ahh....

Yet the veil seems as solid as a wall, as impassable as a mountain in winter, as closed as the mind of a pharisee.

Books and journals, articles and pentacles, and the languid notes of a Satie piano prelude can take me there, may take me there, might take me there, could take me there....

Still....

Awaking from sleep leads to the somnambulance of this quotidian world.

Drifting off to sleep, one awakens to Reality, or (at least) stands at the doorway. A second, third, an infinity of Universes.

You cannot triangulate a position from a single point.

Which brings me back to thoughts of the gatekeeper, who may or may not be listening.

In those dark and solemn shapes under the gray-green water of my mind, in the moment before arising, I sense there is a channel, a pathway, a corridor, a river.

Oh! To stay asleep/awake in the pure, true mystical; she is waiting, ready to reveal to me her marvelous diamond and ambergris Love.

Let me pass!

I have asked and asked again. And I will keep on asking, keep on knocking, keep on....

I am ready for wilder, wetter stories.

I am ready.

Now I lay me down to sleep....

There is more, far more to life than this....

I am ready.

Dinner Companions

"**A** TABLE BY A window, please."

"Certainly, sir."

The maître d' turned.

"Table 477 for Mister Sobel."

Outside, the foggy North Atlantic waters rushed by the ocean liner's windows. Deck 2, close to the water, revealed the growing swells that precede a storm.

After just two meals, the staff brought Judd an iced tea even before they were asked.

Relishing a solitary dinner, an involuntary sigh escaped when Judd saw a couple being steered toward his table. Hopefully, they wouldn't want to make small talk, but....

No sooner had they sat down.

Guten tag. Wie gates?

"Sorry; I speak very little German. *Sprechen sie Englisch?*

Nien. Du nicht sprechen sie Deutsche?

Nien.

So, instead, names were exchanged, and a strained silence ensued.

Wolfgang and Friedel smiled occasionally. Forgetting the language difference, they began to ask something, only to quietly trail off.

The meal was served one course at a time. Small talk consisted of forks scraped on fine china. Meaningful conversation was impossible.

Just as well….

Solid German couple, meet Judd Sobel, American mutt.

Italian on his mother's side. On his dad's, an amalgamation: Quakers, Pennsylvania Dutch, and French Huguenot, eventually marrying Ukrainian Jews.

Judd's Jewish ancestors had come to the United States in the 1880s on steamer ships along with millions of others—the tired, the poor. Settling in New York City, they generally thrived, starting businesses, becoming labor organizers or doctors.

Judd once met ancient relatives who had emigrated later. Three distant cousins who had survived the war...sisters Sadie, Esther, and Gertrude.

Barely five foot tall before the stoop of years set in, wizened and wise, their good humor and gentle natures belied the numbered tattoos on their forearms.

Judd never asked about their past. They had never volunteered. Hence, their stories were long ago lost in the mists of time....

Meanwhile, on a parallel plane of the multiverse:

Guten tag.

Tag. Wei gehts?

Sprechen Sie Englisch?

Ja. "Hi. I'm Judd."

"I am Wolfgang; this is Friedel my wife. You are sailing this your first time?"

"Yes. You?"

"*Ja,* we also. You are American?"

"Yes, born in the States, but my family comes from all over. I'm an American mutt."

All three laughed, although later the Germans would look up the meaning of "mutt," thinking it was related to the German word *mutti* or mother.

The small talk flowed as easily as the ocean, past the windows and under the hull of the great ocean liner.

Unbeknownst to the three acquaintances, others slowly joined them at their table. Hungry ghosts stood pitifully around the Germans, while throngs of emaciated souls in rags mingled on Judd's side.

One, Wolfgang's great-uncle Helmut, in a tattered dull green uniform, rifle slung over his shoulder. At his side, a snapping Doberman, noiselessly barking, baring ghostly teeth.

Over dessert and coffee, the three chatted easily. In the gathering mists, a line formed. The three young sisters clung, desperate to stay together. They filed past the table as Uncle Helmut barked orders....

She Lives

IN THERE.

The night nurse whispered, pointing down a long hall. A lone guard snored easily, as if *he* were nestled in a luxury suite bed.

Opening that door would reveal whether my next story would be a bombshell, or a bomb….

A year ago, I was grinding out column inches on unremarkable, unmemorable news stories. Reporting is like an assembly line conveyor-belt. It never stops.

An event. You gather "facts." Write quickly. Hope you get it right.

Then your story goes up on the website and into print. Or not.

Another event comes down the conveyor. The old, forgotten; the new now your highest priority.

A daily slog, occasionally invigorating, often stultifying.

Then….

Winter last year. A random email. I shouldn't have opened it. We get lots of spam and phishing. But I did.

The subject line, two words:

SHE LIVES

Inside, a link:

www.gonebutnotforgotten.ch

What? Who lives? I debated: Delete and move on or click the link.

Click.

A grainy color photo. A woman propped up in bed. Perhaps sixty? Her expression blank. Unmistakably once a great beauty.

Looking vaguely familiar. Who was she?

White sheets. Brown blanket. Light blue gown. Hospital gown? Bedside table. Lamp. Some kind of picture on the wall. Flowers. Not much else.

News stories came and went. Once in a while, I'd pull up the photograph and stare. The mysterious *SHE LIVES* haunted me.

Then one day, something jumped out. Something that had escaped me before. In the picture over the bed, a faint reflection. A palimpsest lightly overlaid.

My paper keeps forensic image consultants on retainer. "Can you enhance a photo's reflection on glass?"

"Of course."

A few hours later….

"I did some pixel interpolation, noise reduction, and deblurring." The sharpened image came into focus.

"Next time send me a challenge."

The reflection was now clear: three mountains, so distinctive I recognized them immediately. The woman's face clearer, too….

Impossible.

Unbelievable. Too crazy to tell anyone yet, so….

I begged a week's vacation, booked a flight to Zurich, rented a car, and drove to where the photo *must* have come from.

Mayenfeld, in the shadow of the Graubünden Alps. The mountains, Schwarzhorn, Falknis, and Gleghorn. Anyone familiar with the children's book *Heidi* would know these peaks.

The mystery woman *must* have a view of them, a view best seen from the Grand Resort, a spa that since 1242 has catered to the very wealthiest families.

I made inquiries, showed the photo. Blank stares, heads shaking. Some were nervous, some outright refused to look.

Then, the night nurse. She found me at the Kuppelwieser Café. It was *she* who had sent me the photo.

Her story about the woman in the photo, too far-fetched, I needed to see for myself.

That night, she smuggled me into the Grand Resort. The guard snored. I quietly opened the door to see for myself.

Her! She lives!

I knelt. "Your Royal Highness."

No reaction. No response. Blankness couldn't hide her radiant splendor.

Diana Spencer. I cried.

The Unknown Girl
of the Seine

IN PARIS, THE Seine's slow, deep
waters hold stories lost in the
mists of time. Its legendary allure

draws people to its *quais*, quiet spots to dream, to laze, or to fish.

Its banks are places to find romance, of whatever kind. Or they're a jumping off place, out of one life into the next....

The Seine is named for the Sequana tribe who lived near her headwaters. *Une sein* is a net to catch fish and not coincidentally, *le sein* is the French word for "bosom."

Once upon a time, a net had to be strung across the river at St. Cloud below Paris to catch stray bodies, drifting unfortunates. Floating corpses were so common then they were unremarkable.

One night, a lovely young woman drowned and was brought into *la Morgue* behind Notre Dame. The midnight morgue attendant who received the body fell in love with her beauty. She *was* remarkable.

That night, he surreptitiously fashioned a death mask, using grease to coat her placid face, then Plaster of Paris to mold her features.

Word of the Unknown spread quickly through Paris. The *rues*, *passages*, *cul-de-sacs*, *allées* and *boulevards*, the *salons* and *cafés* were abuzz with gossipy news of the sublime beauty, now on display on a slab at the Paris Morgue. A popular amusement in those days, soon lines formed around the building. Everyone flocked to see her.

Who was she?

Would anyone claim her?

Where did she live?

How did she die?

Where was she found, exactly?

Was she a prostitute?

A *grisette*?

An orphan?

And why was she smiling?

Seeing an opportunity, the attendant made copies of the death *masque*, which sold quickly. Shops and salons displayed the *masque* on their walls.

All Paris swirled with speculation. Poets and composers wrote of her life, of her enchantment, of her mystery, of her bliss in death.

Her fame spread, for a time. Then….

The world turned. She drifted out of polite society and into obscurity.

Decades passed until, unexpectedly in Norway....

A young boy. Nearly drowned. In a stream. Saved by his father, the Toymaker.

Tragedy averted, the Toymaker desired to save others.

He consulted experts (medical and scientific) who asked, "Could you make a mannequin to teach people artificial respiration?"

Of course.

He would. He did.

The Toymaker's doll was marvelous, and it worked! He would save lives with this new thing: artificial respiration.

The doll Annie was perfect. Except her visage. Too flat. Not lifelike. What to do?

At his mother-in-law's home, hanging on the wall, the *masque*, vestige of the time when *she* was all the rage.

Here was Annie's face!

Rushing home, he gave the Unknown Girl of the Seine a new life.

Saving lives.

Kissed by millions, her journey took her from the waters of the Seine to a life reviving those who have drowned.

"Annie, are you okay?" CPR students learn to ask. In his song, "Smooth Criminal," Michael Jackson, inspired by Annie, poses the same question,

Art. Saves. Lives.

The Bell

HE WAS FOUR, just turned five, when he tried to ring the bell.

Everything was new. Clothes, new. Yellow school bus, new. Chuck the bus driver was old, but new. The building was old. The teachers were old, and the milk tokens smelled like sour milk.

His haircut was new. Being away from his mother was new, except for the time she and Dad went to the City for a show overnight and his grandparents came to sit.

His shoes were new, and they were brown, and his suit jacket was brown the first day of school with a big yellow tag with all his information on a piece of string looped around the top button.

The black and white picture of his neighbor Sammy Daniels and him in front of the house—they looked like two refugees fresh off the boat.

Sounds were new, the bell rang loudly, and *you shan't be late,* Mom said, tucking some Dentyne gum in his pocket *for later.*

All the kids were new (except Sammy). Mrs. Susan was not new, and ready to retire from teaching, and it showed.

I think I'll have some gum. He thought fondly of Mom. A cross between Doris Day and Lucille Ball, Mom meant well, which often wasn't enough, especially in his later teenage years, when she went off galivanting to the City with her not-so-secret-boyfriend. The whole town knew....

Dentyne is cinnamon-sweet, and sugarless, so no harm could come to you....

Are you chewing??

Um, he ummed, spitting the offending, barely chewed wad into Mrs. Susan's hand. Yuck!

No chewing in school! Go to the corner.

Hot tears of embarrassment, he plotted revenge in the corner....

But that was September, and this was December, and they made paper

Christmas decorations—silver bells and red Santas and green Christmas trees.

And there would be an *assembly* the day before Christmas vacation, which sounded very big and important.

He had never even *heard* of an *assembly*. That was new.

Every class would participate. The morning kindergarteners, too.

Mrs. Susan announced their part would be "Jingle Bells." Not singing it but ringing it!

Mrs. Susan produced a box with bright, pastel-colored bells.

She handed them out. His was baby blue, a big "D" embossed on it.

They practiced ringing, each in turn. *Ring-ring-ring, ring-ring-ring, ring* **Ring** *ringringring*....

The day was cold, clear blue sky, and the snow wasn't old enough to be dirty. Mom brought him to school, instead of the yellow school bus.

All the mothers were there, and the other classes. Kindergarten went first.

All lined up. Christmas-y cherubs. Mrs. Susan, her back to the parents in the gym that served as a cafeteria with a stage for *assemblies*, raised her hands:

Ring-ring ring, ring-ring-ring, ring.

He knew his part. *Here it comes —* he would ring that D loud!

Ring....

The bell rang loudly!

And flew from his hand, skidding across the floor, past Mrs. Susan, toward the parents.

Laughter.

Mixed with hot tears of embarrassment.

About the Author

John Frederick is (or has been) an author, poet, musician, photographer, ordained minister, travel guide, spiritual student, spiritual guide, hus-  band, father, grandfather, politician, chef, legislator, pool player, teacher, and pronoic dreamer.

He is the author of *Paris Histories and Mysteries* and *Prosperity Now! A 12-Week Journey to the Life of Your Dreams*.

Also a singer-songwriter, John's first EP, *Paris Cowboy*, is available on Pandora, iTunes, Spotify, Napster, and many other streaming platforms.

John is currently living the life of his dreams in Paris, France, with Manny and Erica, his teacup Yorkies.

Other Books by John Frederick

Prosperity Now! A 12-Week Journey to The Life of Your Dreams

Are you living the life of your dreams?

If not, why not?

I can just hear your reasons: I've got a kid. I've got a mortgage. I've got parents. But some-day I will....

Stop with the excuses. It's time to answer that question with a resounding "Yes!"

John Frederick has discovered a spiritual path to living the life you want, and in this new book based on his popular course, he will lead you to the life of your dreams.

Are you asking, "How?" As John reveals, you don't even need to ask how. The Universe will supply the "How." You are simply responsible for supplying the dream, believing in your dream, and making the decision to manifest it.

Using ancient and modern spiritual principles, *Prosperity Now!* will guide you through a twelve-week journey to the life of your dreams. You will learn how to discard old, false, and negative ideas in exchange for uplifting, positive, and powerfully practical ideas that work.

Using examples from his own life, John will gently guide you to wake up to this reality: You are worthy and deserving of a fabulous life of your choosing. You can "Begin it now." Change your mind and watch your world transform to meet the new you! It all begins with *Prosperity Now*!

Paris Histories and Mysteries

Who needs another book about Paris? You do!

As much as Paris has been studied, written about, visited, loved, and

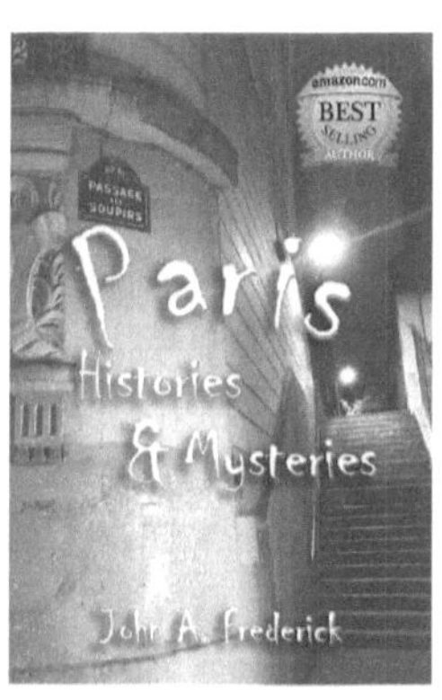

adored, history still has many unanswered questions:

- What would have happened if the contract to demolish the Eiffel Tower had been enforced and Eiffel's lease on the land revoked?

- Who was the "Unknown Girl of the Seine" and how is she still saving people's lives today?

- Was Gaston Leroux's *Phantom of the Opera* a Gothic thriller or an investigative journalist's account of the truth?

- And speaking of investigations, did Edgar Allan Poe—the man who invented the detective story—write the first one in Paris?

- How did an obscure third century saint and martyr inspire a worldwide network of educational institutions?

- How did death appear to people in the Middle Ages, and what happened in Paris to change our way of seeing death and dying?

- Does the alchemist Nicolas Flamel still live and walk the Earth?

Come along and discover a mysterious Paris, one that is more than a tourist stop or a postcard photo-op, but a place where events large and small have altered the course of world history.

Go behind the scenes to discover *Paris Histories and Mysteries*!

All John Frederick's books are available at online booksellers
or ask your local independent bookseller to order them.

Autographed books and CDs are available at:

www.JohnAFrederick.com